'THE SAP, INCENT FEVER, THE DESIRE TO DO, TO ACT, TO ACT THE FOOL, MAKE LOVE, CREATE...'

FRANÇOISE SAGAN
Born 1935, Cajarc, France
Died 2004, Honfleur, France

These stories were first published in French in the collection
Des yeux de soie (1975), which was translated into English as
Silken Eyes and Other Stories (1977).

SAGAN IN PENGUIN MODERN CLASSICS
Bonjour Tristesse and A Certain Smile

FRANÇOISE SAGAN

The Gigolo

Translated by Joanna Kilmartin

PENGUIN BOOKS

PENGUIN CLASSICS

UK | USA | Canada | Ireland | Australia
India | New Zealand | South Africa

Penguin Books is part of the Penguin Random House group
of companies whose addresses can be found at
global.penguinrandomhouse.com.

Des yeux de soie first published by Editions Flammarion in 1975
This selection first published 2018
001

Copyright © Editions Stock, 2009
Translation copyright © André Deutsch Limited and
Dell Publishing Co., Inc., 1977

The moral rights of the author have been asserted

Set in 12/15 pt Dante MT Std
Typeset by Jouve (UK), Milton Keynes
Printed in Great Britain by Clays Ltd, St Ives plc

ISBN: 978-0-241-33964-0

www.greenpenguin.co.uk

Penguin Random House is committed to a
sustainable future for our business, our readers
and our planet. This book is made from Forest
Stewardship Council® certified paper.

Contents

The Gigolo

He walked beside her along the rain-sodden paths full of dead leaves, giving her his hand now and again to guide her round a puddle. He smiled as he did so, a genuine, unforced smile. It occurred to her that this walk in the woods round Meudon would have been a penance for any young man, especially with a woman of her age. Not an old woman, but a bored, jaded one who walked through the woods without any real pleasure, merely because it was preferable to the cinema or a crowded bar.

Of course, for him, there had been the drive there, in the luxurious fast car which it gave him a childish pleasure to drive; but was that sufficient compensation for this interminable, silent walk along these desolate autumnal paths? 'He's bored, he must be bored to death.' Strangely relishing the idea, she turned down another path, one which led them further away from the car, with a sort of dread mixed with hope – the hope that he would suddenly revolt against this boredom, lose his temper, say something wounding, unforgivable, anything that would underline the gap of twenty years between them.

But he always smiled. She had never known him irritable or rude, never seen him smirk in the ironical, condescending way of very young men who know they are desirable. The smirk which said so plainly: 'All right, as a favour to you . . . But remember, I'm as free as air: so don't irritate me.' The cruel smirk of youth which had made her cold, hard and wounding, and had so often caused her to end an affair. With Michel, for instance, the first time she had noticed it, then the others . . .

'Careful,' he said, taking her arm, saving her from tearing her stockings or her dress, her well-cut elegant dress, on a bramble. If he should ever smirk like that, would she still be able to throw him out like the rest of them? She didn't feel she would have the heart. Not that she respected him more than the others: she kept him completely, dressed him, gave him expensive presents which he didn't throw back in her face. He never went in for th stupid, boorish ploys the others indulged in, those sulky moods when they wanted something or felt they were the injured party in the bargain struck between their bodies and her money – that was it, really: they felt hard done by. They would get her to buy them all manner of luxuries and expensive trinkets which they didn't even want, simply in order to restore their self-esteem. The word esteem made her laugh inwardly. It was none the less the only word for it.

Perhaps Nicholas's charm lay in the fact that he really hankered after these presents; not that he demanded them, but he took such evident pleasure in receiving them that she felt like a normal woman rewarding a child instead of an ageing mistress buying a fresh young body she secretly despised. She quickly dismissed such thoughts. Thank God, she didn't go in for being maternal and protective with that bunch of grasping young men who were too handsome for their own good. Neither did she go in for disguising the facts; she was cynical and clear-headed, and they knew it and respected her for it,

dgingly. 'You give me your body, I pay
ome, piqued at not having to rebuff her,
o introduce a vague touch of sentimental-
... ps in order to get a little more out of her.
These she had sent to other protectresses, explaining
to them exactly where they stood: 'I despise you, as
I despise myself for putting up with you. I only keep
you for the sake of those two hours at night.' She
relegated them to the rank of animals, deliberately,
without a qualm.

With Nicholas, it wasn't so simple: he brought no
trace of affection, or caddishness or sentimentality
to his role as gigolo. He was friendly, polite and a
good lover, not very expert, perhaps, but passionate,
almost tender . . . He stayed at home all day, lolling
about on the carpet, reading anything he could lay
his hands on. He didn't ask to be taken out all the
time, and when they did go out he seemed to be
unaware of the meaningful looks they attracted: he
was as attentive and smiling as if he were escorting
the young woman of his choice. In fact, apart from
the condescension, the brutality with which she
treated him, there was nothing to distinguish their
relationship from that of an ordinary couple.

'Aren't you cold?' He glanced at her anxiously as though her health really mattered to him more than anything else in the world. She felt exasperated with him for playing his part so well, for being so nearly what she might still have hoped for ten years ago; she remembered that at the time she still had her rich husband, her rich and ugly husband, whose business affairs were his sole preoccupation.

How could she have been so stupid as to have failed to take advantage of her beauty, now faded, and been unfaithful to him? She had been asleep and it had taken her husband's death and her first night with Michel to awaken her. Everything had begun that night.

'I asked you if you were cold.'

'No, no. Anyway, it's time we went back.'

'Wouldn't you like my jacket?'

His beautiful Creed jacket . . . she glanced at it without interest as at some dull new possession. A russet and grey check, its autumn colours suited Nicholas's thick, silky auburn hair.

'How autumnal we are,' she murmured to herself. 'Your jacket, this wood . . . my autumn.'

He didn't reply. She was surprised at herself

5

because she never alluded to her age. He knew perfectly well how old she was and he didn't care. She might just as well throw herself into that lake. She imagined herself for a moment, floating in the water in her Dior dress . . . Thoughts like that were all very well for the young. 'At my age, one doesn't think of death, one clings to life.' One clings to the pleasures of money, of the night; one makes the most of things, and of people, such as this young man walking beside one down a deserted woodland path.

'Nicholas,' she said, in her hoarse, imperious voice. 'Nicholas, kiss me.'

They were separated by a puddle. He looked at her for a moment before stepping over it, and the thought flashed through her mind: 'He must hate me.' He took her in his arms and gently raised her head.

'My age,' she thought, as he kissed her, 'just for the moment you've forgotten my age; you're too young to play with fire without getting burnt, Nicholas . . .'

'Nicholas!'

He looked at her, a little breathless, his hair rumpled.

'You were hurting me,' she said with a faint smile.

They walked on in silence. She was surprised at the quickening of her pulse. That kiss – what had come over Nicholas? – that kiss was like a farewell kiss, hungry and sad, as if he loved her. He was as free as air; women and luxuries were his for the asking. What had possessed him? And that sudden pallor . . . He was dangerous, extremely dangerous. They had been together over six months; it couldn't go on any longer without leading to trouble. Besides, she was tired, tired of Paris, of the noise and rush. Tomorrow she would leave for the Midi, alone.

They were back at the car. She turned to him and took his arm in an automatic gesture of pity. 'After all,' she thought, 'the poor boy's losing his livelihood. Even if it's only temporary, it's a nasty blow.'

'I'm leaving for the Midi tomorrow, Nicholas. I'm tired.'

'Will you be taking me?'

'No, Nicholas, I shan't be taking you.'

She almost wished that she was; it would have been fun showing Nicholas the sea. He must have been there before, of course, but he always gave the impression of discovering everything for the first time.

'You've had enough of me?'

He spoke softly, his eyes downcast. There was a break in his voice which touched her. She had a glimpse of the life he would have, the sordid quarrels, the compromises and the boredom, all because he was too handsome, too weak and the ideal prey for a certain kind of woman belonging to a certain milieu and with a certain income, women like herself.

'I haven't had enough of you in the least, my dear Nicholas. You're very sweet, very attractive, but it couldn't go on for ever, could it? It's over six months since we met.'

'I know,' he said, as though his mind were elsewhere. 'The first time was at that cocktail party of Mme Essini's.'

She suddenly remembered that hectic party and the first glimpse she had had of Nicholas, looking miserable because old Mme Essini was talking to him at very close quarters and giggling girlishly. Nicholas was pressed up against the bar, with no hope of escape. The scene had amused her at first, then she had looked at Nicholas with increasing interest and cynical speculation. These cocktail parties were like horse fairs or cattle shows. One almost expected to see mature ladies lifting the young men's upper lips to examine their teeth.

Finally, she had gone over to greet her hostess, and passing before a mirror, had suddenly been struck by her own beauty. Nicholas's relief at the interruption had been so obvious that she couldn't help smiling, and her smile had put old Mme Essini on her guard.

She had introduced Nicholas with reluctance. Then there had been the usual gossip about people and their private lives. Nicholas seemed rather at sea. After an hour, she found him decidedly attractive and resolved to tell him so at once, as was her wont. They were sitting on a sofa by a window, and he was lighting a cigarette when she addressed him by name in a voice that scarcely faltered:

'I find you very attractive, Nicholas.'

He made no response, but took the cigarette out of his mouth and gazed at her.

'I live at the Ritz,' she went on coldly.

She was well aware of the importance of this last point. The Ritz was the answer to every gigolo's

9

dream. Nicholas made a slight gesture of protest, but said nothing to show that he had understood. She thought: 'Well, that's that,' and rose to her feet.

Nicholas got up too. He was rather pale.

'May I escort you home?'

In the car, he had put his arm round her shoulders and asked her innumerable eager questions about the overdrive and the finer points of the engine. In the bedroom, it was she who had kissed him first, and he had taken her in his arms with a slight tremor and a mixture of violence and gentleness. At dawn, while he slept like a child, dead to the world, she had gone to the window to watch the day break over the Place Vendôme.

Thereafter, it had been Nicholas playing patience on the floor, Nicholas by her side at the races, Nicholas's eyes on the gold cigarette-case she gave him, and Nicholas suddenly seizing her hand during a party and kissing it. And now there was Nicholas whom she was about to leave and who said nothing, who was keeping up this pose of exaggerated indifference . . .

*

She got into the car and threw her head back, suddenly exhausted. Nicholas got in beside her and drove off.

From time to time on the way back she glanced at his preoccupied, distant profile, and could not help thinking that she would have been madly in love with him at twenty and that maybe life was nothing but a hopeless mess. When they reached the Porte d'Italie, Nicholas turned to her:

'Where are we going?'

'We have to drop in at Johnny's Bar,' she said. 'I've made a date with Mme Essini there for seven o'clock.'

Mme Essini was punctual as usual. It was one of her few virtues. Nicholas shook the old lady's hand, looking rather distraught.

Watching them both, a pleasing idea came to her:

'By the way, I'm leaving for the Midi tomorrow, so I shan't be able to come to your party on the sixteenth. I'm so sorry.'

Mme Essini regarded them both with a bogus air of affection:

'You lucky things, off to the sun . . .'

'I'm not going,' said Nicholas shortly.

There was a silence. The eyes of both women converged on Nicholas, Mme Essini's the more meaningfully.

'Then you must come to my party. You can't stay in Paris all alone, it's too depressing.'

'What a good idea,' she interjected.

Mme Essini's hand was already resting possessively on Nicholas's sleeve. The latter's reaction was unexpected. He jumped up and walked out. She found him waiting by the car.

'What's come over you, Nicholas? Poor old Essini might have been a bit premature, but she's fancied you for a long time, there's nothing to get upset about.'

Nicholas stood there without a word and seemed to be breathing with difficulty. She felt an upsurge of pity.

'Get in. You can tell me all about it when we get home.'

But he didn't wait until they got home. He told her in a strangled voice that he wasn't an animal to be bought and sold, that he could perfectly well look after himself and that he refused to be put out to pasture with an old vulture like Essini. And in any case he couldn't do anything for her, she was too old . . .

'But my dear Nicholas, she's my age.'

They had arrived. Nicholas turned towards her and suddenly took her face between his hands. He looked at her searchingly and she tried in vain to free herself, conscious that her make-up had probably not survived the day.

'You're different,' said Nicholas in a low voice. 'You're . . . you're attractive. I like your face. How could you . . .'

There was a note of despair in his voice as he let her go. She was dumbfounded.

'How could I what?'

'How could you offer me to that woman? Haven't I spent six months with you? Didn't it occur to you that I might become attached to you, that I could . . . ?'

She turned away brusquely.

'You're cheating,' she said in a low voice. '*I* can't afford to cheat. I've had enough. Go away.'

Alone in her bedroom, she examined herself in

13

the mirror. She was irretrievably old; she was over sixty and her eyes were full of tears. She packed hurriedly and went to bed alone in her double bed. She cried for some time before going to sleep, putting it down to nerves.

The Unknown Visitor

She took the corner at full speed and pulled up sharply in front of the house. She always sounded her horn on arrival. She didn't know why, but every time she arrived home she would give David, her husband, this warning that she was back. That day, she found herself wondering how and why she had acquired the habit. After all, they had been married for ten years, they had been living for ten years in this charming cottage in Berkshire, and it hardly seemed necessary to announce herself in this way to the father of her two children, her husband and ultimate protector.

'Where can he have got to?' she said in the ensuing silence, and she got out of the car and walked with her golfer's stride towards the house, followed by the faithful Linda.

Life had not been kind to Linda Forthman. At the age of thirty-two, after an unhappy divorce, she had remained alone – often courted, but still alone – and it required all Millicent's good nature and enthusiasm to endure, for example, this entire Sunday in her company, playing golf. Though uncomplaining, Linda was infuriatingly apathetic. She looked at men (unmarried men, of course), they looked back at her, and things never seemed to go any further. To a woman like Millicent, who was full of charm and vitality, Linda Forthman's character was an enigma. From time to time, with his usual cynicism, David would offer an explanation: 'She's waiting for a chap,' he would say. 'Like every other girl, she's waiting for some chap she can get her hooks into.' Not only was it untrue, it was grossly unfair. In Millicent's view, Linda was simply waiting for someone who would love her, for all her apathy, and take her in hand.

Come to think of it, David was very contemptuous and acerbic on the subject of Linda, and indeed of the majority of their friends. She must talk to him about it. For instance, he refused to see the good side of that buffoon Jack Harris, who, even if he was as dumb as an ox, was generosity and kindness itself. David was always saying of him: 'Jack's a ladies' man . . . without the ladies', at which point he would roar with laughter at his own joke as though it were one of the inimitable witticisms of Shaw or Wilde.

She pushed open the door into the drawing room and paused, flabbergasted, on the threshold. There were overflowing ashtrays and open bottles all over the place and two dressing gowns lying in a corner in a heap: hers and David's. For one panic-stricken moment she wanted to turn round and leave, and pretend not to have seen. She cursed herself for not having telephoned beforehand, to say she was coming back earlier than expected: Sunday night instead of Monday morning. But Linda was there behind her, wide-eyed, a look of dismay on her pale face, and she would have to think up some plausible explanation for the irreparable occurrence that had evidently taken place in her house. Her house . . . ? Their house . . . ? For the past ten years, she had said 'our house' and David 'the house'. For the past ten years, she had talked about pot plants, gardenias, verandahs and lawns, and for the past ten years David had said nothing in reply.

'What on earth,' said Linda, and her high-pitched voice made Millicent shudder, 'what on earth has been going on here? Has David been giving parties in your absence?'

Millicent laughed. She, at least, seemed to be taking it fairly lightly. And indeed it was perfectly possible that David, who had left for Liverpool two days before, had come back unexpectedly, spent the night there and gone out to dine at the near-by Country Club. Only there were these two dressing gowns, those two gaudy shrouds, those two banners, as it were, of adultery. She was astonished by her own astonishment. After all, David was a very attractive man. He had blue eyes, black hair and considerable wit. And yet it had never occurred to her, she had never had the slightest presentiment, let alone proof, that he was interested in any other woman. Of that much, without knowing why, she was certain. In fact she was absolutely convinced that David had never even looked at another woman.

She pulled herself together, crossed the room, picked up the two incriminating dressing gowns and threw them into the kitchen – hurriedly, but not hurriedly enough to avoid seeing the two used cups on the table and a butter-smeared plate. She shut the door hastily as though she had witnessed a rape; and, emptying the ashtrays, tidying away the bottles, chatting amiably, she set about trying to distract Linda from her initial curiosity and get her to sit down.

'Such a bore,' she said. 'Probably the maid didn't come to clean up after last weekend. Do sit down, darling. Shall I make you a cup of tea?'

Linda sat down gloomily, her head between her knees and her bag swinging from her fingertips.

'If you don't mind,' she said, 'I'd prefer something stronger than tea. That last round of golf exhausted me . . .'

Millicent went back to the kitchen, averting her eyes from the cups, grabbed some ice cubes and a bottle of whisky and set them down in front of Linda. They sat facing one another in the drawing room furnished in bamboo and shadowed cretonne which David had brought back from somewhere or other. The room now looked – if not human – at least presentable once again, and through the french windows the elm trees could be seen swaying in the wind, that same wind which had driven them off the golf course an hour ago.

'David's in Liverpool,' said Millicent, and she realized that her voice was peremptory, as though she felt poor Linda was liable to contradict her.

'I know,' said Linda amiably, 'you told me.'

They both stared out of the window, then at their feet, then at one another.

Something was beginning to take hold in Millicent's mind. Like a wolf, or a fox, at any rate some sort of wild animal, it was gnawing at her. And the pain was getting worse. She gulped down some whisky to calm herself and caught Linda's eye again. 'Well,' she thought to herself, 'if it's what I think it is, if it's what any reasonable person might be expected to think it is, at least it isn't Linda. We've been together all weekend and she's just as appalled as I am, in fact even more so, oddly enough.' For, to her mind, the idea of David bringing a woman back to their house, whether or not the children were there, the idea of David bringing that woman here and lending her her dressing gown, still seemed absolutely unthinkable. David never looked at other women. In fact David never looked at anyone. And the word 'anyone' suddenly resounded in her head like a gong. It was true that he never looked at anyone. Not even her. David had been born handsome and blind.

Of course it was natural enough, only seemly, really, that after ten years their physical relations should have dwindled practically to nothing. Of course it was only to be expected that after all this time nothing much should remain of the eager, hot-blooded, highly-strung young man she had once known, but even so it was really rather odd that this handsome husband of hers, so blind but so attractive . . .

'Millicent,' said Linda, 'what do you make of all this?'

She gestured vaguely around the room, indicating the general disorder.

'What do you expect me to make of it?' said Millicent. 'Either Mrs Briggs, the charlady, didn't come in last Monday to clean up, or else David spent the weekend here with a call-girl.'

And she laughed. If anything she felt rather relieved. These were the two alternatives, there was no great mystery about it. There was nothing wrong with having a good laugh with a girl friend about being deceived by one's husband and discovering it by chance because it was too windy to play golf.

'But,' said Linda (and she too was laughing), 'but what do you mean, a call-girl? David spends his entire time with you and the children and your friends. I can't see how he would have the time for girls.'

'Oh, well,' said Millicent, laughing even louder – she really did feel relieved, without knowing why – 'perhaps it's Pamela or Esther or Janie . . . Search me.'

'I don't think any of them would appeal to him,' said Linda, almost regretfully, and she made a move as if to get up, to Millicent's alarm.

'Look, Linda,' she said, 'even if we had caught them in the act, you know very well we wouldn't have made a scene. After all, we've been married for ten years, David and I. Both of us have had the odd fling . . . there's nothing to make a fuss about . . .'

'I know,' said Linda, 'these things don't matter very much. All the same, I must go, I want to get back to London.'

'You don't like David much, do you?'

For a second there was a look of amazement in Linda's eyes, which quickly changed to one of warmth and tenderness.

'Yes I do, I like him very much. I've known him since I was five years old, he was my brother's best friend at Eton . . .'

And, having made that pointless and uninteresting statement, she looked intently at Millicent, as though she had just said something of the utmost importance.

'Good,' said Millicent. 'In that case, I don't see why you can't forgive David for something I myself am prepared to forgive. I know the house is in a mess, but I'd rather stay here than be stuck in that awful traffic all the way back to London!'

'David is very good to you,' she said.

'Of course he is,' said Millicent unhesitatingly.

And it was true that he had been a considerate husband, courteous, protective and on occasion highly imaginative. He could also, alas, be exceedingly neurotic: but she would keep that to herself. She wasn't going to tell Linda about David lying on the sofa in London with his eyes closed for days on end, refusing to go out. She wasn't going to tell her about

David's terrifying nightmares. She wasn't going to tell her about David's manic telephone conversations with some businessman whose name she couldn't even remember. She wasn't going to tell her about David's rages when one of the children failed an exam. Nor would she tell Linda how insufferable David could be about furniture or pictures, nor how forgetful David, the considerate David, sometimes was about his appointments, including those with her. Nor about the state he was sometimes in, when he came home. Least of all could she tell Linda about the marks she had seen on his back one day when she caught sight of it in the mirror . . . And the mere memory of this was enough to break down her conventional English reticence, and she asked – at least she heard herself ask – 'Do you really think it's Esther or Pamela?' Because it was true that he didn't have the time to see other women, and even women who indulge in illicit affairs demand a certain amount of time from their lovers. David's adventures, if they existed, could only be crude, frantic, hurried affairs, with prostitutes or specialists. And it was surely impossible to imagine David, proud, fastidious David, as a masochist . . .

Linda's voice seemed to come from a long way away.

'What makes you think of Pamela or Esther? They're much too demanding . . .'

'You're right,' said Millicent.

She stood up, went over to the mirror on the wall and examined herself in it. She was still beautiful – men had told her so often enough, and sometimes proved they meant it – and her husband was one of the most charming and gifted men in their circle. Why, then, did she seem to see in the mirror a sort of skeleton without flesh or nerves or blood or sinews?

'It seems a pity,' she said (she hardly knew what she was saying any longer), 'it seems a pity that David hasn't more men friends, as well as women friends. Have you noticed?'

'I've never noticed anything,' said Linda, or rather Linda's voice, since dusk had descended and all Millicent could see of her was a silhouette, a sort of mouse-like creature perched on the sofa, who knew – but what did she know? The woman's name. Why didn't she tell her? Linda was nasty enough or nice enough – how could one tell in such cases? – to murmur a name. Why then, in this July twilight, wrapped in her solitude and her pale suit, did she look as though she was scared out of her wits? One must be rational and down to earth about these things. If it was true, she would have to face up to the fact that David was having an affair with some woman, either a friend or a professional. Vulgar recriminations must be avoided at all costs, and, perhaps, later on, she might even take a light-hearted revenge with Percy or someone. One must see things in their proper perspective, like a woman of the world. She got to her feet, straightened the cushions with a regal hand, and declared:

'Listen, darling, whatever happens we'll stay here the night. I'll go and see what sort of state the rooms are in upstairs. If by any chance my husband has been having an orgy, I'll telephone Mrs Briggs, who lives down the road, and ask her to give us a hand. Does that suit you?'

'Fine,' said Linda from the shadows. 'Fine. Anything you say.'

And Millicent walked towards the staircase, giving the photograph of their sons an absent-minded smile on the way. They were to go to Eton, like

David, and who else was it? Oh, yes, Linda's brother. Climbing the stairs, she was surprised to find that she needed to lean on the banisters. Something had deprived her of the use of her legs; it wasn't the golf, nor the thought of possible adultery. Anyone can envisage, indeed must envisage, the possibility of their partner's infidelity – it wasn't an excuse for creating a scene or putting on an act. Not to Milli-cent's way of thinking, at any rate. She went into 'their' bedroom, the bedroom of 'their' house, and noticed without the slightest embarrassment that the bed was unmade, the sheets rumpled, churned up as they had never been, it seemed to her, since her marriage to David. Then she noticed the watch on the bedside table, *her* bedside table. It was a heavy, waterproof watch, a man's watch, and she weighed it in her hand for a moment, fascinated and incredulous, until the realization that it must have been left behind by another man finally sank in. She understood everything now. Downstairs, there was Linda, worried stiff and getting more and more scared, sitting there, in the dark. Millicent went down-stairs again, and with a curious, almost pitying expression in her eyes, looked at dear Linda who also knew.

'Linda, my poor pet,' she said, 'I'm afraid you were right. There's a pair of salmon-pink cami-knickers in the bedroom I wouldn't be seen dead in.'

The Lake of Loneliness

Prudence – for such was her name, alas, and an inappropriate one at that – Prudence Delvaux had parked her car in a forest ride, near Trappes, and was strolling aimlessly in the damp, chill November wind. It was five o'clock and growing dark: a melancholy hour, in a melancholy month, in a melancholy landscape, but nonetheless she whistled as she walked, stooping now and then to pick up a chestnut or a russet leaf whose colour appealed to her. She wondered drily what she was doing there – why, on her way home from a charming weekend, with charming friends, with her charming lover, she had felt a sudden and almost irresistible urge to stop her Fiat and set off on foot on this heart-rending autumn evening, why she had suddenly succumbed to the desire to be alone and walk.

She was wearing a silk scarf and an extremely well-cut coat in lodencloth the colour of the leaves, she was thirty years old and her hand-sewn walking shoes made every stride a pleasure. A rook flew cawing overhead and was immediately joined by a bevy of its fellows until they filled the sky to the horizon. And oddly enough, this raucous cry, familiar though it was, made her heart beat faster as though in response to some nameless terror. Not that Prudence was afraid of prowlers, or the cold, or the wind, or even of life itself. On the contrary, her friends would burst out laughing whenever they uttered her name. Considering her attitude to life, they said, it was the purest paradox. However, she hated anything she couldn't understand, and that was really the only thing she was frightened of: not understanding what was happening to her. And now, suddenly, she had to stop and catch her breath.

The landscape reminded her of a Breughel, and she liked Breughel; she liked the warm car that awaited her and the music she would switch on once she was back inside it; she liked the thought of meeting, around eight o'clock, a man who loved her and whom she loved in return, a man called

Jean-François. She also liked the thought of getting up, yawning, after their night of love, and gulping down the cup of coffee which he, or she, would have made for 'the other'; and also the thought of her office tomorrow morning, of discussing advertising ideas with Marc, the good friend with whom she had worked for the past five years. They would agree, laughing, that in the end the best way of promoting a new washing powder was to show that it washed greyer, and that people needed greyness more than whiteness, dullness more than sparkle, obsolescence more than durability.

She liked all that; in fact, she liked her life: plenty of friends, plenty of lovers, an amusing job, a child even, together with a taste for music, books, flowers and log fires. But now this rook had flown over, chased by that frantic rabble, and something was tearing at her heart, something that she couldn't quite grasp, couldn't explain, not even (and this was the worst part) to herself.

The path branched to the right. There was a noticeboard proclaiming '*Etangs de Hollande*'. The idea of those lakes in the setting sun, with reeds, furze, perhaps some duck, immediately attracted her

and she quickened her step. She came upon the first
of the promised lakes almost at once. It was a mixture of blues and greys, and although not covered
with wildfowl (there wasn't even a single duck) it
was nevertheless strewn with dead leaves which
were slowly sinking, one after another, in a dying
spiral; and each one seemed to be in need of aid and
protection. Each of these dead leaves was an Ophe-
lia. Spotting a dead tree trunk, no doubt abandoned
by a careless forester, she sat down on it. Increasing-
ly, she asked herself what she was doing there. She
would end up by being late, Jean-François would
be worried; he would be furious and he would be
quite right. When one is happy, when one is doing
what one likes to do – and also when other people
like one – one has no right to sit about on tree
trunks, alone, in the cold, beside a lake no one has
ever heard of. It wasn't as though she was at all 'neurotic', as 'other people' say when talking of unhappy
people (or at any rate, people who couldn't cope
with life).

As though to reassure herself, she took a packet of
cigarettes from her coat pocket, was relieved to dis-
cover a lighter in the other pocket, and lit up. The

smoke was warm and acrid, and the cigarette tasted unfamiliar. And yet it was the same brand that she had been smoking for ten years.

'Perhaps,' she said to herself, 'all I really needed was to be alone for a bit? Perhaps it's too long since I've been alone? Perhaps this lake has an evil spirit? Perhaps it wasn't chance but fate that led me here? Perhaps there's a long history of charms and spells surrounding these lakes . . .'

She put her hand on the tree trunk at the point where her hip rested against it, and felt the contact of the rough wood, worn and mellowed by rain and by solitude (for what could be more solitary or more melancholy than a dead tree, cut down, abandoned, no good for anything; not as firewood, nor as timber, nor as a lovers' seat?). The contact with the wood aroused a sort of tenderness and affection in her, and to her astonishment she felt the tears well up in her eyes. She contemplated the wood, the veins of the wood, difficult though they were to make out: grey, almost white, in wood that had itself turned grey and white (like old people's veins, she thought: one can't see the blood flowing, one knows it's there but one can't see it any more than one can hear it).

And it was much the same with this tree: the sap had dried up; the sap, the incentive, the fever, the desire to *do*, to *act*, to act the fool, make love, create, make things happen . . .

All these ideas went through her head in a flash; resigned, passive, she hardly knew who she was any longer. She, who never saw herself, who never even wanted to see herself, whose life was full, now suddenly saw herself as a woman in a smart coat, smoking a cigarette, sitting on a dead tree trunk beside a stagnant lake. There was someone inside her who wanted desperately to get away from this place, to go back to the car, to the music in the car, to the road and the thousand and one ways of avoiding death, the thousand and one tricks a clever motorist must know to avoid accidents, someone who longed to be back in Jean-François's arms, or in a Paris café with 'the gin, the gipsies, the siphons and the garishness' so dear to the heart of Guillaume Apollinaire. But there was someone else inside her whom she didn't recognize – at least whom she had never met until now – who wanted to stay until nightfall, watching the darkness settle on the lake and feeling the wood grow cold beneath her hand. And perhaps – why not – this someone would later want to walk into that water, aware of the cold at first, then, immersing herself in it, losing herself in it, go down to the deepest depths to rejoin, on the blue and golden sands, the dead leaves which had been sucked down there throughout the day. And there, stretched out on a bed of leaves, surrounded by tender, playful fishes, this someone would be perfectly at peace at last, restored to the cradle, restored to real life, or rather to death.

'I'm going crazy,' she thought, and a voice whispered to her: 'I assure you it's the truth, your truth,' and it seemed to be the voice of childhood. And another voice, a voice acquired over thirty years of pleasure of one kind or another, said, 'My dear girl, what you ought to do is to go home and take some Vitamin B or C. There's something the matter with you.'

Needless to say, it was the second voice which prevailed. Prudence Delvaux stood up, abandoning the tree trunk, the lake, the leaves and life. She returned to Paris, to her divans, her bars, to what is known as existence. She returned to her love, who was known as Jean-François.

And she switched on the music in her car and she drove very carefully and she even smiled at her half-hour of aberration. But it took her two months to forget the *Etangs de Hollande*. At least. And not once did she mention them to Jean-François.

In Extremis

He turned over yet again between the enveloping sheets, dangerous as quicksands, sniffing with disgust the smell of his own body, that smell he had once so delighted to find on women's bodies in the morning. Those mornings in Paris after a white night and a few hours of exhausted sleep beside a strange body, those mornings when he awoke light-headed with fatigue and in a hurry to leave. In a hurry . . . he had always been a man in a hurry, but now, on this spring afternoon, lying there prostrate, he was taking his time about dying. Dying was a strange word, no longer, it seemed to him, the absurd but inescapable reality which had so often spurred him on, but a sort of accident. Rather like breaking a leg skiing. 'Why me, why today, why?'

'Of course I may recover,' he said out loud. And the shadowy figure silhouetted against the window gave a slight start. He had forgotten her, as indeed he had always forgotten her. He remembered his surprise on learning of her affair with Jean. There was someone for whom she still existed, was still beautiful, for whom she had a body. He gave a faint chuckle which quickened his precious, precarious heart-beat.

He was dying. He knew now that he was dying. Something was tearing at his body. Meanwhile she was leaning over him, supporting him by the shoulders, and he felt his shoulder-blade, ignominiously reduced to skin and bone, flinch beneath his wife's gentle hand. Ignominy, that was what he was dying of, ignominy. Was there an illness which allowed you to die gracefully? There probably wasn't, and mankind's only grace, perhaps, lay in that aspiration towards what lay ahead. But he was calmer now, and as she leant over him to lay him back on his pillow, her face caught the light and he saw her. She had a beautiful face, all said and done, for which he had married her twenty years earlier. But its expression irritated him. It was preoccupied, abstracted. She must be thinking of Jean.

'I was saying that I might perhaps recover.'

'Of course you will,' she said.

It was funny: she really didn't love him any more. She knew perfectly well that he was lost, done for. But it was such a long time ago that 'she' had lost him. 'One only loses people once.' Where had he read that? Was it true? At all events, she would never again see him come through the door, read his newspaper, talk. No, she no longer loved him. If she had loved him, she would have taken his hands and said: 'Yes, my darling, you're going to die,' with that smooth, drawn face that comes from the knowledge of the irrevocable, the knowledge that one acquires all of a sudden when faced with somebody one loves who is dying, somebody . . .

'You mustn't get agitated,' she said.

'I'm not agitated, I'm just a little restless. Agitation is over as far as I'm concerned.'

He had adopted a playful tone. 'But after all, I'm going to die,' he thought, 'perhaps I ought to talk to her seriously? But what about? About us? But there's nothing left to talk about, or hardly anything.' Nevertheless, the mere thought that he could still exert some influence by his words brought back his old impatience.

'I'll do my best,' he said. 'I'm sorry.'

And he reached for her hand with a calm deliberate gesture. The last time had been two years ago, in the Bois de Boulogne: he was sitting on a bench with a young and rather silly girl and he had made the same calm gesture, in order not to alarm her. Pointlessly, as it turned out, for she was back at his flat with him an hour later. But he remembered the immense length of time it had taken before his hand reached those slightly reddened fingers . . . It was moments like those . . .

'You have nice hands,' he said.

She didn't reply. He could hardly see her. He would have liked her to open the shutters, but it occurred to him that darkness was more appropriate to this final act of the play. Play? What gave him that idea? There was nothing theatrical about his situation. But he was doing his best to remedy that.

'It's Thursday today,' he said plaintively, 'half-holiday. When I was a small boy, I always hoped that a week with four Thursdays in a row would turn up one day. I do now: then I'd have three days longer to live.'

'Don't talk nonsense,' she said with an impatient shrug.

'Oh no you don't!' he said, suddenly furious, trying to raise himself on his elbows. 'You're not going to do me out of my death! You know perfectly well that I'm going to die.'

She looked at him with a slight smile.

'Why are you smiling?' he asked in a gentle voice.

'That reminded me of a remark you made – you probably won't remember it – about fifteen years ago. We were at the Faltoneys. I didn't know that you were being unfaithful to me at the time, or at any rate I only had a faint suspicion . . .'

He felt the stirrings of an old complacency that he quickly suppressed. What extraordinary situations he had got himself into, what unbelievable adventures he had had!

'Well, go on.'

'That evening I realized that you were Nicole Faltoney's lover. Her husband wasn't there, and when you brought me home, you said you had to drop in at your office to finish something or other . . .'

She spoke slowly, pausing after every other word.

His thoughts had turned to Nicole. She was blonde, gentle, a little querulous.

'So then I said that I'd like you to come home with me, that I'd prefer it if you did. I didn't dare tell you that I knew: you were always talking about the stupidity of jealous women, and I was afraid . . .'

She spoke more and more softly, dreamily, almost like someone tenderly recalling an unhappy childhood. It got on his nerves.

'You mean I told you I was going to die?'

'No, but you used much the same formula: you said . . . Oh, no!' she said, and she burst out laughing, 'it's too preposterous . . .'

He began to laugh too, but half-heartedly. It scarcely seemed the moment for laughter, especially not for her – only he could be allowed such heroic gaiety.

'Well? Go on.'

'You said: "You're not going to deprive me of that woman, you know perfectly well that I want her."'

'Oh,' he said. (He was disappointed, having vaguely expected some witticism.) 'There's nothing very funny about that.'

'No,' she said. 'But to say that to me, as though it was self-evident! . . .'

She laughed again, but with a touch of constraint, as though she sensed that he was annoyed.

But now he was busy listening to his heart. Its beat was muffled, pitifully faint. 'How frail we are,' he thought with a touch of bitterness. He was tired of seeing clichés he had despised at the age of twenty being borne out time and again. Death was going to resemble death just as much as love resembled love.

'Ah, well,' he said, closing his eyes, 'it's been a very accommodating heart.'

'What?' she said.

He looked at her. It was strange to be leaving behind one a person primed with such anecdotes, stories against one, against what would be one's ghost. Someone who had been so gentle at twenty, so defenceless, and whom he now found so changed – whom he would never find again. Marthe . . . Whatever had become of her?

'Do you love this man Jean?' he asked.

She answered him, but he wasn't listening. He was trying for the umpteenth time to count the sunbeams on the ceiling. The wavering, feathery reflections of the sun. Would the Mediterranean still be as blue, afterwards? Someone was singing in the courtyard. He had loved a handful of songs in his life so passionately that, in the end, he could no longer bear to listen to music. Marthe, on the other hand, used to play the piano. But pretty pianos were hard to find and he had been very particular when it came to furniture. So they hadn't had a piano.

'Don't you play the piano any longer?' he asked plaintively.

'The piano?' she said wonderingly.

She was surprised; she herself couldn't remember any more: she had forgotten her youth. He alone retained the fond memory of Marthe's blonde hair and straight young neck against the black background of the piano. He turned his head away.

'Why do you ask me about the piano?' she asked again.

He didn't reply, but he squeezed her hand. His heart frightened him; he recognized the old pain. He longed for a moment's reassurance, the comfort of Daphne's shoulder, the taste of alcohol.

But Daphne was living with that young idiot Guy

and alcohol would only hasten the end. He was afraid, that was all, simply afraid . . . It was that blankness in his head and that shrinking of his muscles. It was horrible. The thought of his death filled him with such horror that it made him smile.

'I'm afraid,' he said to Marthe. Then he repeated the words, stressing each syllable. They were harsh, rough words, manly words. All the words in his life had been so easy to say, tripping off the tongue: 'my darling, my sweet, whenever you like, soon, tomorrow.' Marthe wasn't a very soft name and it hadn't come often to his lips.

'Don't worry,' she said.

Then she leaned over him and put her hand over his eyes.

'Everything will be all right. I shall be here. I won't leave you.'

'Oh, it doesn't matter,' he said, 'if you have to go out, if you've some shopping to do . . .'

'Later.'

Her eyes were full of tears. Poor Marthe, crying didn't suit her. Nevertheless, he felt a little comforted.

'You don't feel bitter towards me?' he said.

'I remember other things too,' she said, dropping her voice to a whisper that reminded him of a dozen similar, slightly breathless voices in the corner of a drawing room or on a beach. His coffin would be followed by a long trail of whispers, tender and silly. Sitting at home in her armchair, Daphne, the last of his mistresses, would evoke his memory, much to Guy's irritation.

'All is well,' he said. 'I should have liked to die in a cornfield, though.'

'What do you mean?'

'With the wheat waving over my head. You know the line: "the wind is rising, life must go on".'

'Calm yourself.'

'The dying are always told to keep calm. A fine time to say it.'

'Yes,' she said, 'it's the right time.'

He thought what a beautiful voice she had. He was still holding her hand in his. He would die with a woman's hand in his; all would be well. What did it matter if the woman was his own wife? 'Happiness between two people,' he said, 'it's not so easy.'

Then he burst out laughing, because, in the last resort, he didn't give a damn about happiness. Happiness, or Marthe, or Daphne. He was nothing but a heart still beating away, and that, for the moment, was the only thing that mattered to him.